Star the Snow

Michael began to feel
excited as he looked at the parcels
with his name on them. He
picked up as many of his presents
as he could carry and made for
the door. But just as he was going
out of the room, Michael heard a
strange noise.

Miaooww!

Michael was so surprised he
dropped some of the parcels he
was carrying. He put the rest of
them down and began to look for
where the noise was coming
from . . .

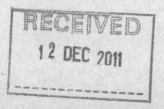

Titles in Jenny Dale's KITTEN TALES™ series

1. Star the Snowy Kitten
2. Bob the Bouncy Kitten
3. Felix the Fluffy Kitten
4. Nell the Naughty Kitten
5. Leo the Lucky Kitten
6. Patch the Perfect Kitten
7. Lucy the Lonely Kitten
8. Colin the Clumsy Kitten
9. Poppy the Posh Kitten
10. Snuggles the Sleepy Kitten
11. Pip the Prize Kitten
12. Sid the Speedy Kitten

All of Jenny Dale's KITTEN TALES books can
be ordered at your local bookshop or are
available by post from Book Service by Post
(tel: 01624 675137)

Jenny Dale's KITTEN TALES™

Star the Snowy Kitten

by Jenny Dale

Illustrated by Susan Hellard

A Working Partners Book

MACMILLAN CHILDREN'S BOOKS

To Maisie – a star in her own right
Special thanks to Mary Hooper

First published 1999 by Macmillan Children's Books
a division of Macmillan Publishers Limited
20 New Wharf Road, London N1 9RR
Basingstoke and Oxford
www.panmacmillan.com

Associated companies throughout the world

Created by Working Partners Limited
London W6 0QT

ISBN 0 330 37451 6

7 9 8

A CIP catalogue record for this book is available from
the British Library.

Typeset by SX Composing DTP, Rayleigh, Essex
Printed and bound in Great Britain by Mackays of Chatham plc, Kent

Chapter One

Michael knelt down beside the fire in his gran's flat and ruffled Archie's fur. The big tabby cat began to purr.

"I wish Archie could come and live with us," Michael said.

"Don't be silly," Mrs Tappin, his mum, replied. "What would

Gran do without him?"

Michael put his head down onto Archie's tummy. "I'd love a kitten of my own even more."

His mum and gran looked at each other and raised their eyebrows.

Michael closed his eyes and wished. *I really hope I get a kitten for Christmas.*

It was Christmas Eve and Michael and his mum had just popped in to see his gran. Archie, her cat, was dozing in front of the electric fire.

Archie was old now, with raggedy fur. Once he'd been lean and active, but now he was large and soft, his body sprawled out like a bag of knitting.

"I thought you wanted a mountain bike!" Michael's gran said. Michael opened his eyes. "I'm *saving* for a mountain bike," he replied. "I've been saving for ages. But I'd like a kitten for my Christmas present."

"You got a kitten last Christmas," his mum reminded him.

"But that wasn't a real one," Michael argued.

Because he'd kept on about kittens so much, one of Michael's presents last year had been a toy kitten, with fluffy ginger fur and curly whiskers. He now sat on the shelf above Michael's bed. Sometimes, when no one was looking, Michael gave him a cuddle.

"You're too young to look after a real kitten yourself," Mrs Tappin said.

"I still want one," said Michael. "I'll *always* want one."

"They cost a lot of money, kittens do," said his gran. "There's food and vet's bills."

"And cat baskets and flea

collars!" Mrs Tappin put in.

"But Archie doesn't cost you much, does he, Gran?" Michael asked. He stroked the pale fur on Archie's tummy, which was soft as feathers.

"Not now," his gran replied. "He doesn't need a lot of fuss and expense. All he needs now is a laze in front of the fire and a snooze." She smiled. "Like me!"

Michael put his face close to Archie's and touched the tip of the cat's damp, pink nose with his own. Archie's whiskers quivered and one ear twitched slightly. "Did he play a lot when he was younger? Did he do naughty things?" he asked.

"Oh, my goodness, yes," said

his gran. "He used to run up these curtains quicker than a rat up a drainpipe!"

"One Christmas he climbed the tree!" Michael's mum put in. She nodded towards the funny old plastic Christmas tree that his gran put up every Christmas. It was a bit bent and a bit bare. But she said she liked it like that.

"That's how it got bent," said his gran.

Michael looked at Archie's crumpled, sleeping face. "Oh, *please* let me have a kitten!"

Michael's mum and gran looked at each other again.

"You'll have enough money for your bike soon," Mrs Tappin said. "Then you won't want to stay in with a kitten."

"I will," said Michael. "I'll have plenty of time left for a kitten."

Michael's gran walked over to the window. "It said on the news that it's going to snow," she said. "We might have a white Christmas this year!"

Michael looked up. "That would be great!" Then he sighed, and leant down to scratch the soft furry folds around Archie's neck. "But not as great as having a kitten," he said quietly to himself.

On the way home, it began, very gently, to snow. A few flakes circled the street lights and fluttered to rest on Michael's anorak.

Chapter Two

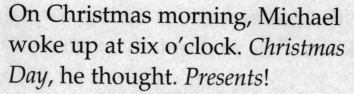

On Christmas morning, Michael woke up at six o'clock. *Christmas Day*, he thought. *Presents!*

It was still dark but there was a strange glow coming through the curtains. Michael jumped out of bed to have a look. He pulled back the curtain. "Snow!" he breathed.

There was snow everywhere: on the road, in the gardens, along the roofs of the houses opposite.

Michael had never seen so much snow. "Oh, wow!" he said. Part of him wanted to dash out and build a snowman. But then . . . Christmas was waiting!

There, in the shadows by the bottom of his bed, Michael saw his stocking. It was bulging with presents! Full of excitement, Michael dragged it up and tipped everything out onto his bed.

All the parcels were wrapped in silver and gold. Michael tore off the wrapping to find all sorts of goodies. His favourites were a box with a black cat on it and a book about kittens.

Right at the bottom of the
stocking, in its toe, Michael found
a handful of chocolate coins
covered in gold foil. He peeled
four of them, crammed them in
his mouth and then pulled on a
jumper, ready to race downstairs.

Under the tree in the sitting
room, he knew he'd find his big

presents. He still hoped that there might . . . just possibly . . . be a kitten.

Downstairs, the sitting room was lit by the same soft glow as Michael's bedroom. Under the tree, parcels of all different shapes, colours and sizes had arrived, as if by magic. But Michael couldn't see a kitten.

For a moment he felt disappointed.

"Michael!" his mum called from upstairs. "We can hear you!"

"Come up and show us your presents!" his dad said.

Michael began to feel a little bit excited again as he looked at the parcels with his name on them.

"Coming!" he called back. He picked up as many of his presents as he could carry and made for the door. But just as he was going out of the room, Michael heard a strange noise.

Miaooww!

Michael was so surprised he dropped some of the parcels he was carrying. He put the rest of them down and began to look for where the noise was coming from.

He looked under the sofa, under the table and chairs, and behind the sideboard. But no luck.

He looked behind the bookcase and out in the hall. He still couldn't find anything. Perhaps he'd imagined it.

Miaaowww!

But there it was again! And it was coming from outside . . .

Michael ran over to the curtains and pulled them open. The garden was blanketed with snow.

And there, pressed up against the glass door that led to the back garden, was a small black kitten. A very snowy kitten.

"Oh!" Michael cried. He opened the door and scooped up the kitten in his arms. "What are you doing out there in the snow?"

Holding the bedraggled black bundle against the warmth of his jumper, Michael shivered and quickly closed the door. "I wonder who you belong to?" he whispered.

The kitten looked up at Michael with bright green eyes, then mewed.

And to Michael, it seemed she was saying, "I belong to you!"

Chapter Three

Very quietly, Michael crept upstairs to his bedroom. He put the kitten on his bed and covered it with a fold of duvet to keep it warm.

He stroked its soft damp fur, hardly able to believe it. A kitten, waiting for him on Christmas morning!

The kitten was black, except for a white, star-shaped mark that stretched from nose to chest.

"I'm going to call you Star," Michael decided. He thought the kitten looked like a girl. He tickled her tiny pointed ears. "You're my Christmas Star!"

The kitten began to purr softly,

and rubbed a tiny black cheek against Michael's hand.

"Michael, what *are* you doing?" came his dad's voice.

"Almost there!" Michael called back. He didn't dare tell his mum and dad about Star. They might not let him keep her. No, he'd have to hide her for the time being. And then, after Christmas, he'd think about what to do.

Michael bent to kiss Star's soft forehead. "I'll be back as soon as I can, Star," he whispered. "I'll bring you something to eat."

Quietly, Michael left his bedroom and went downstairs to pick up some of his parcels again.

"Happy Christmas!" his mum and dad said as he went into their bedroom. "Let's see your presents."

There were some great things in Michael's parcels – a computer game, a video and two more books from his favourite animal series. There was also a safety lock, a horn and some lights for his bike – and some money from his gran towards buying it!

"So are you pleased, love?" Mrs Tappin asked, smiling.

Michael nodded. "They're all brilliant!" he said happily. *Especially my secret present*, he thought to himself.

Later that morning, Michael's mum and dad were getting suspicious. Usually Michael spent Christmas morning downstairs, playing with his new toys and watching TV, but today he'd spent a lot of time upstairs in his room.

"Do you feel all right?" Mrs Tappin asked. "One minute you're here, next you're gone! You've hardly looked at your new bike stuff. I don't think you've even opened your books!"

"I feel great!" Michael replied. "I'm just going upstairs to . . . to write some thank-you letters."

His dad looked at him with astonishment. "Are you *sure* you feel all right, Michael?"

"Course I do!" Michael said, then he ran up to his room and closed the door behind him.

Snuggled in Michael's duvet, Star was snoozing. Earlier,

Michael had brought her up a bowl of breakfast cereal, mashed up with lots of milk. She'd eaten every bit; then, with a round, full tummy, she'd fallen fast asleep. Michael was planning to bring her some turkey later.

Suddenly the kitten's eyes opened. Seeing Michael, she began to purr madly.

Michael gently ruffled the fur around her ears. "Are you ready to play, now?" he asked. He trailed a piece of tinsel that he'd picked off the Christmas tree across the duvet.

As she caught sight of it, Star's green eyes opened wide. She leapt to her feet, then crouched, ears pricked, quivering all over

as she prepared to pounce.
Suddenly she leapt on the
moving tinsel, attacking it with
tiny paws and teeth.

Michael laughed out loud. Then
his face grew more serious. "I
don't know what to do about you
going to the loo, Star," he said.

"You're going to want to go soon, now you've woken up." He looked around his room thoughtfully. Star put her head to one side, watching his every move. "I think I'd better put some newspaper under the bed and then you can—"

Suddenly, Michael's door opened and his mum stood in the doorway. Her eyes widened as she saw Star. "Where did you . . . Where has that kitten come from?" she gasped.

Michael ran over and scooped up Star. "She was outside!" he said. "This morning, when I got up to open my presents, she was outside in the snow."

"I don't believe it!" Mrs Tappin

said faintly. She sat down on the bed. "Clive," she called to Michael's dad, "come quickly!"

Mr Tappin came hurrying in. He too stopped still in the doorway when he saw the kitten in Michael's arms.

"She's mine!" Michael said fiercely. "I wished for a kitten and Star came along!" He held her close. "You will let me keep her, won't you?" he pleaded.

Mrs Tappin sighed. "I'm sorry, love," she said. "She belongs to someone else. Kittens don't just turn up on your doorstep like magic."

"And whoever she belongs to will be missing her," Mr Tappin added. "We'll have to put her outside again so she can go back to her real home. It's only right." Michael hugged Star even tighter.

"Think how you'd feel if you had a kitten and it just disappeared," his mum said gently.

Michael nodded slowly.

"She'll find her way back to where she came from," Michael's dad reassured him. "But you must say goodbye to her now."

When his mum and dad had left the bedroom, Michael put his head down on Star's fluffy tummy. His wish had come true: he'd got a kitten for Christmas. But now she was being taken away . . .

Chapter Four

"Anyone for second helpings?"
Mr Tappin asked. The family
were sitting at the dining table,
eating Christmas lunch.

   Michael's granny always came
to lunch on Christmas Day, with
Archie. She puffed out her
cheeks. "No thanks, love,

I'm full," she said.

"If I ate anything else I'd go pop!" said Mr Tappin.

"How about you, Michael?" his mum asked.

Michael shook his head, a great lump in his throat. He'd managed to eat some of his Christmas lunch, but he hadn't enjoyed it half as much as he usually did. He was too worried about Star.

After the kitten had been put back out into the snow, she'd hung around the door for a while, miaowing – then she'd disappeared. Michael's mum and dad had said she'd gone home. But Michael wasn't so sure.

"So – who's for Christmas pudding?" Mrs Tappin asked

next. Mr Tappin groaned. "Or shall we wait a while?" she added hastily.

"Good idea," Michael's gran said as she sank down on the sofa next to Archie.

Suddenly Michael heard a familiar mewing sound. He turned to look over at the glass door. "Look! Star's come back!" he shouted.

Everyone looked towards the garden. Star stood there in the snow, her fur sticking up in damp spikes. She mewed again, then started scratching at the glass.

"So that's the little thing you've been telling me about!" said Michael's gran.

Michael nodded, then looked

at his mum, hopefully.

Mrs Tappin stood up. "If we ignore her, I expect she'll go home. Now, does anyone want a mince pie?"

"But, Mum!" Michael pleaded. "She'll be freezing cold out there. It's starting to snow again. The snow will get so deep that it will go right over her head."

"Cats are very sensible . . ." his mum began, and then she looked at Star and hesitated. "Oh, dear," she said. "She does look a bit wet, doesn't she?"

"And it is Christmas . . ." said Michael's gran, winking at him.

"Perhaps just for a little while, then," Mrs Tappin agreed. "Until we can find her owners . . ."

Before they could say anything else, Michael was opening the door and lifting the shivering kitten into his arms. "You came back!" he said, holding her close to him and not caring a bit about his Christmas jumper getting wet.

Mrs Tappin went to get an old towel from the kitchen to dry Star.

Archie seemed to sense that there was something going on and woke up from his snooze. Raising his head, he spotted the tiny intruder, jumped down from the sofa and stood at Michael's feet staring up. He gave a loud, loud miaow. Who was this cheeky young thing?

"You can be introduced in a minute," Michael's gran said.

"The youngster needs to be dried first."

Mrs Tappin gave Michael the towel and he sat by the fire with Star on his lap. Very gently he patted her wet fur, rubbing under her tummy where she was wettest of all.

As her fur got dry and fluffy, Star curled round and round on Michael's lap, loving all the attention. Purring non-stop, she put out her tongue and began to lick Michael's hand.

"It feels all tickly," he laughed. He was so happy! He'd wanted a cat for ages . . .

While he'd been drying the kitten, the family had been watching, and now they all thought Star was really sweet.

But *someone* didn't think she was very sweet. Archie stood on red alert, ears pricked and eyes wide, watching the stranger's every movement.

Michael's dad told him to put Star down next to the older cat.

"I hope they'll be friends," Michael said anxiously, lowering Star to the floor.

The big tabby cat and the tiny black kitten stared at each other. Their noses twitched as they sniffed unfamiliar scents and their tails swung slowly from side to side. They were weighing each other up.

Star took a timid step closer to Archie, but Archie immediately

gave a low growl of disapproval.
He raised his back into a high
arch and fluffed up his raggedy
fur.

Star shrank away, scared.
Michael moved in to pick her up
and protect her. He wasn't going
to have his little kitten frightened!

"They'll be friends all in good

time," said Michael's gran.

"I expect the little thing's hungry," Mrs Tappin said. "Maybe she wants her Christmas lunch."

Michael nodded eagerly. "Oh, yes, please," he said. "If you give me some turkey, I'll chop it up for her. And can she have some gravy on it?"

His mum laughed. "I suppose you want the gravy warmed up?"

"Yes, please," Michael said.

Mrs Tappin returned with Star's food and gave it to Michael. He put it down in the middle of the floor and sat down right beside her to watch her eat it.

Star munched away, her tiny

white teeth flashing and her pink tongue hungrily licking up the gravy.

"Look at her eat!" Mr Tappin said. "Anyone would think she'd never seen a Christmas lunch before."

"She hasn't!" Michael said, and then realised that his dad was joking.

Archie had some turkey too, of course, and when both cats had finished their meal they sat by the fire. They didn't look at each other but sat carefully licking round their mouths and smoothing their whiskers with their paws.

"I think they're going to be friends," Michael said. He

beamed at his gran. "Archie can be Star's grandad!"

The three grown-ups looked at each other.

"Don't forget, love," his mum said, "Star might not be here for long. She belongs to someone else. You're just borrowing her."

Michael didn't answer. He watched his lovely kitten, not wanting to miss a lick of her paw or a swish of her tail.

When she'd finished washing, Star stretched and yawned widely. Michael thought she was about to fall asleep but she suddenly leapt right over the dozing Archie and made a beeline for Michael's dad. She ran straight up his trousers, across his

jumper and round the back of his neck.

Mr Tappin gave a shout of surprise. "She's climbing onto my head!"

Everyone started laughing.

"It looks like you're wearing a furry scarf!" Michael's gran said.

"Aren't kittens fun!" Michael said, happily.

"Yes, they are," said his mum. But then her face turned serious. "But Michael, you must remember that Star isn't really yours."

Michael pretended not to hear her again. Star was his. She *was* . . .

Chapter Five

"Now, what shall we say on this poster?" asked Mr Tappin.

It was three days after Christmas and he and Michael were sitting at his computer. They'd contacted the RSPCA and the local vet to report that they'd found a kitten, and now they were making a poster.

"I don't know," Michael said. He didn't want to be helpful.

"I suppose we should start off by describing her," said his dad. "Black kitten with white star-shaped mark on her chest . . ."

"What if no one claims her?" Michael asked.

"Don't build your hopes up," Mr Tappin replied. "Someone must be really worried about her."

There was a scratching at the door. Michael went over to open it and Star padded into the room. She rubbed her head against his ankle, purring loudly.

Michael picked Star up and took her to sit with him. The kitten seemed very interested in the computer and leapt from Michael's lap onto the table.

Zedtonimplurr appeared on the screen as she stepped daintily across the computer keyboard.

"Out of the way, naughty puss," said Mr Tappin, laughing.

Star blinked up at him, giving her cutest look. "Mia–oww!"

zedtonimplurr

Michael's dad grinned. "She is a sweet little thing," he said. "I'll miss her when she goes."

"So will I," said Michael, picking her up and hugging her. *Oh, please*, he thought to himself, *please don't let anyone claim her . . .*

That afternoon, Michael and his dad went round the village, putting up the posters:

KITTEN FOUND ON
CHRISTMAS DAY
BLACK, WITH WHITE STAR-
SHAPED MARK ON HER CHEST
Please contact: 8 Harshaw Villas
Telephone: 0126 545 593

"I think we only need to put up

one or two posters," Michael said.

"No, we'll need a few more than that," said Mr Tappin. "Maybe ten or twelve."

"I'll do them," Michael said quickly. "You can go home."

Mr Tappin shook his head. "I'm not daft!" he said. "You wouldn't put up any at all if I left you to it, because you don't want anyone to find out we've got Star!"

"I would," Michael said. "But I might put them up back to front," he admitted. "Or I might not push the drawing pin in very hard and they might fall off!"

His dad laughed. "That's why I think I'd better be here."

When they'd put up ten posters, including one in the post office,

they walked home.

Star was sitting on the kitchen window-sill, looking out. When she saw Michael she began to miaow happily.

Michael walked into the kitchen and grinned. "I love having her here, don't you?"

"Yes, I do, love," Mr Tappin said. "But I'm sure the person she belongs to will be searching for her. And they'll soon see one of the posters we've put up."

Michael picked up Star and held her tightly. He just didn't want to think about that.

The phone call came two days later, just as Michael was about to take Star upstairs to bed.

Mr Tappin answered the phone and Michael saw his face grow serious. "I see. Yes, we've got her," he said. "That's right, black, with a white mark on her chest . . ."

Michael began to feel sick.

"Yes, tomorrow morning will be fine," his dad went on. Mr Tappin put down the phone. "That was a Mrs Patel from Dinby Way."

Michael didn't say anything.

His dad shot him a sympathetic glance. "She bought a kitten for her daughter's birthday a couple of weeks before Christmas and it disappeared."

Michael felt like he was going to cry. "No!" he said.

"Mrs Patel said her daughter misses her kitten very much," his dad said quietly.

Michael scooped Star up and ran upstairs to his bedroom. "Star wants to be with me!" he cried as he slammed the door. "They're not having her!"

Chapter Six

"Post, Michael!" his mum called the next morning. "There's something for you from Scotland."

"OK," Michael said gloomily. He and Star were playing with a ping-pong ball, and he kept thinking that this might be the last time they ever played together.

Star put out a velvety paw and swiped the ball – right between Michael's knees. "Goal!" he laughed. "Clever girl!" He rolled the ball for Star one last time. While she scooted after it, Michael went into the kitchen.

His mum held out an envelope to him, smiling. "It's from Scottish Granny," she said.

Scottish Granny, who lived near Aberdeen, always sent New Year cards and presents instead of Christmas ones. Michael usually got a book token from her.

He took the envelope and looked at his watch. Nearly eleven o'clock! He'd been up since before it was light that morning, playing with Star. This time tomorrow, someone else would be playing with her.

"Aren't you going to open the card?" Mrs Tappin asked.

Michael nodded, slit open the envelope and pulled out a New Year card. But it didn't have a book token with it. Instead, there was a cheque – for fifty pounds!

"Oh!" Michael cried. "The rest of my bike money – all at once!"

His mum smiled. "Granny knew you'd been saving hard and wanted to help," she explained.

Michael put the card and the cheque down on the kitchen table. He tried to feel excited. But

really all he could think about
was Star.

He went back into the sitting
room. Star was now curled into a
black fluffy ball, fast asleep
behind the sofa.

Michael crouched down to
watch her. Star's whiskers

twitched gently as she breathed in and out. She looked so sweet that Michael felt as if he was going to cry.

Just then, he heard a noise on the gravel outside. There was a knock at the door. Star opened her eyes and peered up at him.

Mrs Tappin came into the room. "That'll be the people for Star," she said gently. She put an arm round Michael's shoulders. "Be brave, love. You've looked after her very well. And perhaps in a year or so, you can have another kitten – a kitten of your own."

Michael shrugged her arm away. "I don't want another kitten!" he said. He was trying really hard not to cry now.

Michael's dad showed Mrs Patel and her daughter Nashi into the room. Michael thought they looked very nice. But he couldn't like them – they were going to take Star away from him.

"She's behind the sofa," he muttered, then turned away and blew his nose. "She's asleep. She likes sleeping there."

Nashi, a small girl with long plaits, crawled behind the sofa.

Michael held his breath.

After a few long seconds, Nashi crawled out again, looking upset. "It's not her!" she said.

Michael felt the tightness and the tears inside him disappear as if by magic. He let out his breath in a long sigh.

"Are you sure?" Mrs Patel asked.

Nashi nodded sadly. "It's definitely not our Leyla," she said. "Leyla has one white toe, and a bit of white on the end of her tail as well."

Mrs Patel turned to Michael's mum and dad. "Thank you," she

said. "We'll try the vet's next. There's a lost kitten there."

"I really hope you find her," Michael said to Nashi.

Nashi smiled. "Thank you," she said. Then she and her mother went off towards the village vet's.

Michael let out a shout of joy. This made Star jump. She sprang to her feet and, before Michael could catch her, ran straight up Mr Tappin's trouser leg and huddled on his right shoulder.

"Ow!" Michael's dad yelled, hopping around. "Her claws are getting sharper! And she's making holes in all my shirts!"

Star scrambled down his front and pounced on his slippers. What fun!

Michael and his mum couldn't stop laughing. As Star skittered across the wooden floor and hid behind a potted plant, Michael felt so happy, he thought he would burst!

"Well!" Mrs Tappin said.

Then there was a long silence.

"So . . ." said Mr Tappin. "What now?" He scratched his head. "No one else seems to be missing a kitten around here. It's a mystery where she came from."

Star seemed to know something was up. She peeped out from behind the plant, looking from one to the other of them.

Michael took a deep breath. "I'd like to spend my bike money," he announced.

"You want to buy your bike now?" his mum said.

"No . . ." Michael said slowly. "I want to spend the money on Star. She needs injections and a cat basket and a collar and—"

"Yes, that's true," his dad interrupted. "But . . . what about your bike?"

"I still want it," Michael said, "but that can wait. Mostly I want to look after Star. And I thought that if I bought all her things myself you might . . . let me keep her . . . if no one else claims her."

Michael's mum and dad looked at each other. "What do you think, Clive?" Mrs Tappin asked.

"Well," Mr Tappin said seriously, "having watched Michael with Star, I *do* think he'd look after her properly."

"So do I," Mrs Tappin agreed, smiling. "And no one's claimed her . . . so . . ."

Michael flew over to Star, picked her up and held her tightly. "Did you hear that, Star?" he said. "You can stay here, with us!"

Star began to purr and rubbed her face against Michael's chin.

"Oh, by the way, Michael . . ." Mr Tappin said.

"Yes, Dad?" Michael asked.

"All that money you've got – how would you like to buy me some new trousers and shirts?" his dad joked.

"And if you've got any money left over, I'd like a new set of sitting-room curtains, please," Michael's mum joined in. "Star seems to think curtains are there for her to use as a climbing frame!"

As her new family laughed, Star smiled too – though to anyone else it looked like a yawn. Yes,

she thought, she'd chosen her
new home very well. And here
she was going to stay . . .

Collect all of JENNY DALE'S KITTEN TALES™!

The prices shown below are correct at the time of going to press.
However, Macmillan Publishers reserve the right to show new retail
prices on covers which may differ from those previously advertised.

JENNY DALE'S KITTEN TALES™

1. Star the Snowy Kitten	0 330 37451 6	£2.99
2. Bob the Bouncy Kitten	0 330 37452 4	£2.99
3. Felix the Fluffy Kitten	0 330 37453 2	£2.99
4. Nell the Naughty Kitten	0 330 37454 0	£2.99
5. Leo the Lucky Kitten	0 330 37455 9	£2.99
6. Patch the Perfect Kitten	0 330 37456 7	£2.99
7. Lucy the Lonely Kitten	0 330 37457 5	£2.99
8. Colin the Clumsy Kitten	0 330 37458 3	£2.99
9. Poppy the Posh Kitten	0 330 397338	£2.99
10. Snuggles the Sleepy Kitten	0 330 397346	£2.99
11. Pip the Prize Kitten	0 330 397354	£2.99
12. Sid the Speedy Kitten	0 330 397362	£2.99

All Macmillan titles can be ordered at your local bookshop
or are available by post from:

**Book Service by Post
PO Box 29, Douglas, Isle of Man IM99 1BQ**

Credit cards accepted. For details:
Telephone: 01624 675137
Fax: 01624 670923
E-mail: bookshop@enterprise.net

Free postage and packing in the UK.
Overseas customers: add £1 per book (paperback)
and £3 per book (hardback).